This book belongs to:

____

Also by Kitty Michaels

The **Ballet Friends** series

#1 Toe-tally Fabulous

#2 Join the Club

#3 Birthday at the Ballet

#4 Nowhere to Turn

#5 Waiting in the Wings

#6 Dance School Divas

#7 Ballerinas on Broadway

#8 Pageant Prima

#9 The Triple Threats

#10 The Nutcracker Ballet Club

Visit **www.balletfriendsbooks.com** today!

Once Upon a Tutu

Five Ballet Fairy Tales Starring the Ballet Friends

♥♥♥

The Princess and the Prima

Ballerella

Snow Tights and the Seven Dancers

Goldilocks and the Three Barres

The Klutzy Duckling

♥♥♥

Kitty Michaels

Ballet Friends Books
An imprint of Poolside Press

Copyright © 2012 by Kitty Michaels
Ballet Friends™ is a trademark of Kitty Michaels.
All rights reserved.

ISBN: 1-4392-1833-1
ISBN-13: 978-1-4392-1833-4

Ballet Friends Books
An imprint of Poolside Press

Printed in the U.S.A.
Charleston, SC

Visit us on the Web
www.balletfriendsbooks.com

Once Upon a Tutu

Five Ballet Fairy Tales
Starring the Ballet Friends

The Ballet Friends Present

The Princess and the Prima

By Kitty Michaels

Inspired by Mark Twain's
The Prince and the Pauper

Princess Bianca

The Princess and the Prima

Once upon a tutu there was a lovely princess named Bianca. She lived in a magnificent castle in a faraway land. Princess Bianca was the only daughter of King Phillip and Queen Beatrice. One day, she would become Queen and rule her kingdom known as Ridgepoint.

The King and Queen loved their daughter, but kept her locked in the castle to study her royal duties all day and all night. Princess Bianca was an obedient and kind daughter and carried out her parents' every wish.

But Bianca secretly longed to be a prima ballerina. Every night with her head resting on her pillow of silk, and her long blonde hair shining in the moonlight from her window, she dreamed she was dancing ballet on a large stage for all to see.

In her dreams, she always wore a pair of pretty, pink toe shoes made by the Royal Cobbler. They were magical shoes that swept her across the stage and made her feel like she was flying.

But Princess Bianca always awoke to the sound of her tutor's bell, which was followed by the thud of a stack of Princess Books for her daily lesson. She studied Geography before breakfast, Manners during breakfast, History of the Kingdom before lunch, Grace during lunch, Literature and Poetry all afternoon, Music during dinner, and Astronomy until bedtime.

The Princess worked very hard, but on the other side of the kingdom, down a cobble path and over the footbridge, another girl worked very hard, too.

There, in the attic of the Ridgepoint Ballet Troupe, lived a beautiful prima ballerina named Jessica. She was the orphan of two great dancers who died very young. They left their daughter to their trusted friend and ballet teacher, Sir Elliott, who controlled the only ballet school in the kingdom.

Sir Elliott, who was quite short and wore a tall hat, made Jessica practice her dancing all day and perform all night without any breaks.

Young Jessica was the star of every ballet performed in the kingdom. She danced in three or four shows each night and worked her feet to the bone. But she did not complain, for Sir Elliott was her guardian and took her in when she was left without any money or even a crumb to eat.

And then, one sunny spring morning, with the birds chirping in the square and the townspeople selling their fresh breads, cheese, and flowers, fate brought Princess Bianca and Jessica the Prima together.

On a very secret trip into town, and without any guards, Princess Bianca rode on her white horse up to the Royal Cobbler's shop. Wearing a pink coat and a rather plain blue dress, she clutched her royal slippers in her hands.

If anyone asked her why she brought her royal slippers all the way into town, she would say they were torn and needed mending. But only Princess Bianca knew the real reason she brought her royal slippers into town. She was to have them turned into the most magnificent royal toe shoes!

But something, *or someone,* caught Princess Bianca's eye before she could enter the cobbler's shop. Across the way and through an open window of a tall brick house, she spotted a beautiful ballerina leaping through the air.

It was Jessica the prima ballerina! Bianca watched Jessica twirl and leap across the floor over and over, until finally Sir Elliott was called away. Then Jessica was given a very brief break from her rehearsal.

Then to Princess Bianca's surprise, the beautiful prima ballerina stepped out of the hot and stuffy ballet studio for some fresh air. She took a seat on the curb to loosen her pink toe shoe ribbons and give her tired feet a rest.

"You dance beautifully!" called the Princess, as she joined the dancer.

"Thank you," the Prima replied, not even noticing that she was speaking to Princess Bianca, and continued loosening her ribbons.

"I wish I could dance as gracefully as you," said the Princess. "But the King won't allow me."

"Huh?" the Prima asked, now looking up and realizing it was the Princess!

Jessica started to stand up to curtsey, but Princess Bianca immediately stopped her and said:

"No need. You deserve to rest. Please call me Bianca. What's your name?"

"Princess, I mean Bianca, my name is Jessica. Wow, I've never met royalty before. I've danced for them, but I've never met them," the Prima said.

"You mean all these years you've been dancing for audiences, and I've been locked away in the castle? How I wish I could have seen you perform," the Princess sighed.

"Gee, I wish I was in the castle where you were, instead of dancing on my toes day and night. What's it like living in a castle? You must have more than one meal a day, and your food must be hot, isn't it?" asked the Prima.

"Yes, it is hot. And there is more food than I can eat. But with all there is in the castle, it seems so empty. There is no dance, and therefore I can only dance in my dreams," said the Princess.

Just then, Princess Bianca loosened the bow around her neck, and removed the large pink coat she used to disguise herself.

"Wow!" cried Jessica, "I only have one small mirror in my room, but it's as if I'm looking in it right now!"

The Prima was indeed right. The two girls looked like identical twins, and could easily pass for each other!

"Wait, I just had one of my best ideas! You want to be me, right? And I want to be you, right? Well, why don't we? Let's trade shoes!" the Princess cheered, showing her jeweled, pink satin heels.

"Nice princess shoes! They must be real comfy! Yes, let's trade! Here, take my toe shoes, and tie the ribbons real tight. You'll be doing a lot of dancing in those. And I'll gladly live in your castle and fill my belly tonight!" the Prima cheered.

"It's a deal. We'll trade places for three days. Let's meet here in front of the Royal Cobbler's shop at sunset on the third day," the Princess said.

"It's a deal, your Highness," nodded the Prima.

"No, call me *Jessica,*" giggled the Princess.

That night, atop a high hill, and past the royal guards, Jessica the Prima snuck into the castle through a secret entrance that Bianca told her to use. Once inside, Jessica was quickly met by Bianca's young Royal Chambermaid named Megan.

"Oh, your Highness! You're late for your morning History lesson! Come right this way!" the Chambermaid yelped.

"Uh, can't we eat first? Where's the kitchen?" Jessica asked, looking around.

At that very moment, Megan knew something wasn't right.

"Oh my gosh! You're not the Princess! Where is she? What did you do with her? Tell me at once!" Megan demanded.

"Hold your horses. Everything's okay. I'm here on the Princess's orders. We switched places for three days, and you can't tell anyone or the Princess will be mad," Jessica revealed.

"But, but," Megan started.

"Don't worry. I look just like the Princess. How hard could it be to act like a Princess?" asked Jessica.

"You'll find out. You have a test today!" Megan cried, grabbing Jessica's arm and taking her to see the Royal Tutor.

In the meantime, Princess Bianca was taking orders from mean Sir Elliott in the hot and stuffy ballet studio across the street from the cobbler's shop.

"*Bang, bang, bang!*" went Sir Elliott's cane, as he beat it on the floor to count out the dance steps.

"I beg your pardon!" Bianca gasped, rubbing her tired feet. They were sore after dancing for several hours in Jessica's old toe shoes.

"Again! And faster!" he barked, banging his cane on the floor.

Then Bianca shot up onto her toes and stood up as straight as she could.

"*Pirouette!*" Sir Elliott called loudly.

"Huh?" Bianca shrugged, not knowing the ballet term.

"*Huh?*" Sir Elliott scowled back, getting angry.

"Um, that means twirl around," a soft, helpful voice whispered from behind the piano.

"Thank you," Bianca whispered back, and did a graceful twirl.

"Enough!" Sir Elliott called, leaving the room to have his supper.

"Thank you, little girl. You really saved me back there," Bianca said to the tiny girl seated at the piano.

“I’m Lexi. Who are you?” replied the little girl with brown hair.

“You mean you knew? Oh no, what about Sir Elliott?” Bianca worried.

“You fooled him, but you didn’t fool me. You’re not as good a dancer as Jessica. She’s my friend,” Lexi said.

“Well I’ll be your friend, too. Allow me to introduce myself. But first, can you keep a secret?” Bianca asked.

“I love secrets!” Lexi squealed.

“You must swear not to tell anyone my true identity. For I am Princess Bianca, future Queen of Ridgepoint, and hopefully one day, a prima ballerina!”

“Oh, no wonder you’re so pretty!” Lexi called.

“We’ll get along just fine,” Bianca grinned, taking a break and sitting on the piano bench next to Lexi.

Later that same night at the castle, Jessica the Prima met the Queen for the first time at dinner. Accompanied by her new friend and chambermaid Megan, Jessica strolled into the dining room and took a seat at the head of the table.

"That seat's for the King," Megan whispered into Jessica's ear, and pointed to the correct seat across the table where the Princess always sat.

"Oops," Jessica giggled, and moved over to the right seat.

Then she grabbed a loaf of bread and tore a large piece off, and put it right in her mouth. She tucked the rest of it in the pocket of her royal gown, to eat later.

"Ahem!" the Queen called, raising her eyebrow at the Princess.

"Oh, excuse me, Miss Queen," Jessica said, with her mouth full of bread.

"Ahem!" the Queen called louder.

"Mom?" Jessica guessed.

"*Ahem!*" the Queen gasped.

"Your Queenship?" Jessica tried.

"Oh my!" Megan worried, whispering the correct answer into Jessica's ear.

"Mother! That's it!" Jessica cried, snapping her fingers.

"Dear, what has gotten into you today? The tutor said you failed your test. You need to study all night long!" the Queen ordered.

"Yes, Mother," Jessica nodded, and then grabbed a huge hunk of cheese and stuffed it in her mouth to mix with the bread.

"*Bianca?* Where are your manners? The Princess must abide by the strict rules of Princess Conduct at all times and never, ever serve herself, or she will be a huge disgrace on this entire kingdom!" the Queen yelled.

Then Jessica turned to Megan and said, "Gee, this princess stuff isn't a piece of cake like I thought it was."

But just as she was about to help herself to a piece of cake, she stopped herself and signaled to Megan to serve her a large slice of chocolate cake.

The next two days went by quickly, with Princess Bianca dancing ballet just as she had always dreamed, but was missing her family and life at the castle. She was also growing tired of Sir Elliott's constant orders and cold soup and stale bread for her only meal of the day.

On the third day, in the middle of rehearsal, Sir Elliott declared:

"Tonight will be our last performance in Ridgepoint! After the show, we will pack everything up and move on to a foreign land where we shall stay forever!"

"*What?*" Bianca and Lexi both cried together.

"There's no time to talk. Pack your bags and be ready to go right after your final bow. We must leave before sunset!" Sir Elliott called, disappearing into a back room.

"Oh no, before sunset?" Bianca asked, knowing that if she didn't switch back with Jessica the real Prima at sunset, she would never see her family again, and never become Queen of Ridgepoint.

"Don't worry, Princess. I will help you," Lexi promised, putting her hand on Bianca's shoulder.

"But how?" Bianca asked.

"I will go to the castle and find Jessica and bring her back," Lexi decided.

"Oh, then you must use the secret entrance. Find a chambermaid named Megan, and she will lead you to Jessica," Bianca whispered.

"Your wish is my command," Lexi declared, and headed straight for the castle.

After a long and difficult journey on foot, Lexi made her way to the palace gate. She followed the wall around the castle just as Bianca told her to.

Suddenly, Lexi found a secret hole in the wall covered by a tree branch. Then she entered the castle through the hole, without being spotted by the Royal Guards.

"*Eek!*" Lexi cried, as she landed on her bottom, inside the servant's quarters of the castle.

"Who are you, kid?" Megan called, mending her plain, brown dress.

"Um, I'm Lexi from the ballet. I play piano. I need to find someone named Megan," replied Lexi.

"You hit the jackpot, kid! That's me, but I have problems of my own to take care of. Wait a minute, did you say the ballet? Did the Princess send you?" Megan demanded.

"Yes, and she's in trouble! Sir Elliott is moving the ballet company to a faraway land, never to return! And he's going to take the Princess with him unless we do something!" Lexi warned.

"Oh my gosh! We have to switch them back right now! I'll take you to the Princess's chambers!" Megan shrieked.

Then she pulled Lexi down the hall, up ten flights of stairs, down another long hall, up another ten flights of stairs, and finally to the Royal Bedroom.

There they found Jessica sitting on the bed with a mountain of books around her. She was reading her History lesson.

"Jessica, thank goodness!" Lexi cried.

"Little Lexi, is that you? Where's your piano?" Jessica asked.

"Jessica, I missed you!" Lexi called, and ran over to Jessica's side.

"Me too," Jessica said, and hugged little Lexi.

"Listen, Princess Bianca is in really big trouble! We gotta go!" Megan urged, yanking Jessica out of bed, and rushing everyone to the secret exit.

Then the group crawled through the hole in the castle wall, and quickly hopped on Princess Bianca's white horse.

"Everyone hold on!" Megan called, grabbing the horse's reins.

"But I don't know how to ride a horse," Jessica worried.

"Just sit behind me and hold on!" Megan ordered.

"Giddy-up, horsey!" Lexi cried.

They rode all the way into town, and down the long cobblestone path to the theater, where the ballet was to perform for the last time in Ridgepoint.

Just moments before Princess Bianca was to take center stage, she was joined backstage by her Royal Chambermaid Megan, little musician Lexi, and prima ballerina Jessica.

"Oh, perfect timing! Good job, ladies! The show's just about to start! Jessica, take your toe shoes back. It's your turn again," Bianca said.

"No, Princess. Let us dance together tonight!" Jessica called.

The Queen at the ballet

With Megan and Lexi watching from the wings, Princess Bianca and Prima Jessica took the stage, hand-in-hand. They dazzled the audience with their beautiful dancing and graceful steps.

"*Encore!*" called a familiar voice in the audience.

"Mother, is that you?" Princess Bianca asked, squinting to see the Queen in the audience.

Then the Queen spoke again.

"Yes, I followed you here. Only there are two of you! What is going on here?" the Queen demanded.

Then Princess Bianca told her story, and the Queen had only this to say:

"I am very sorry, my dear child. I kept you locked in the castle all these years and did not allow you to dance, which is truly in your heart. From now on, you are allowed to dance whenever you like."

"How wonderful!" Bianca cheered.

"And your new friend, Jessica, is to stay here in Ridgepoint, where she will be the star dancer of Ridgepoint's new Royal Ballet, which shall remain here forever," the Queen declared.

"*Yippee!*" Jessica the Prima cheered, and then added, "Oops, that wasn't very Princess-like of me, was it?"

Then the Princess and the Prima shared a big laugh, but then they both remembered one last thing they needed to take care of.

"What about that mean Sir Elliott?" Princess Bianca asked the Queen.

"Oh yes. Sir Elliott, you are officially appointed to the post of Royal Juggler. You will be sent overseas to entertain our royal troops!" the Queen laughed.

"Oh rats," Sir Elliott frowned, and knew that his days of mistreating Jessica and the other dancers were over.

The Princess and the Prima took their final bows, and Lexi and Megan cheered. And together, the girls stayed best friends in the kingdom of Ridgepoint, and they lived happily ever after.

The Ballet Friends Present

BALLERELLA

By Kitty Michaels

Inspired by The Brothers Grimm's
Cinderella

Poor Ballerella

Ballerella

Once upon a tutu there lived a sweet girl named Ballerella. She lived in a grand manor in the countryside, and lived a happy life with her caring father, until one day he married Stepmother.

With Stepmother came two very mean stepsisters, Jillian and Cornelia, to live in the manor. But soon after the wedding, Ballerella's father grew ill and died, leaving Ballerella in the care of Stepmother.

It was then that Ballerella saw the true colors of her stepfamily.

Stepmother ordered Ballerella to work like a slave in the manor and wait on her stepsisters hand and foot. Ballerella's clothes, which had always been made of fine silks and lace, were now full of holes and filth.

Poor Ballerella spent her long days sweeping the floors, cleaning the chimney, milking the cows, and doing all the cooking and laundry in the house.

Even with all the hard work and unhappiness, there was a bright light in Ballerella's life. Ballerella loved dancing, especially ballet. No one else knew this, but when Ballerella did her chores, she was always dancing in her mind.

When she swept the floors, she pretended as if she was dancing for the King and Queen. And when she scrubbed the windows, she pretended as if the sunlight was a spotlight above the stage shining down on her. She even entertained all of the barnyard animals each morning with the sweet tune of "Swan Lake," which she whistled while she milked Clara the Cow.

But one day, Ballerella's dreams of dancing ballet would come true.

"*Knock, knock!*" went the front door.

"Ballerella! Get the door!" Stepmother ordered.

"Yes, Stepmother," replied Ballerella.

Ballerella opened the door, and there stood the King's Royal Messenger.

"By order of the King, all eligible ballerinas are to perform at tonight's royal ballet performance, in order for the Prince to choose his future Princess," said the messenger.

"Ooh, ooh! I'm going to be the Princess!" Jillian cried out, running down the stairs and jumping for joy.

"No, Jillian! I'm going to be the Princess! I'm the best dancer in the kingdom!" Cornelia claimed, pushing her sister aside and doing a terrible little leap, bumping right into Stepmother.

"Not at this rate, Cornelia. You have two left feet. But that will soon change. I'm hiring the best ballet teacher to come over and teach you girls how to sweep the Prince off his feet," Stepmother said.

"Oh, I can't wait to learn ballet from a real ballet teacher!" Ballerella cheered.

"Nonsense, child. You have chores to do. I believe the roof needs repair," Stepmother barked.

"Yes, Stepmother. I'll go up on the roof at once," replied Ballerella, with a very sad face.

"Ha, ha, ha! Like you could ever dance, Ballerella!" Jillian and Cornelia heckled together, and then left to change into their leotards.

A little while later, when Ballerella was outside the manor and half way up the ladder to the roof, she spotted the ballet class through Jillian and Cornelia's bedroom window.

She watched Madame Simpson's private lesson for Jillian and Cornelia. She studied every step through the window, while balancing on the rickety ladder. She did every move in her mind, just as the graceful Madame Simpson demonstrated. Ballerella was sure she could do those fancy ballet steps.

Determined to go to the royal ballet performance that evening, Ballerella quickly finished her last chore up on the roof, and went to the barn to find some saddle leather.

From a small scrap of leather, Ballerella made her very own ballet toe shoes! She was all set to dance that evening, until she realized that she had no ribbon for her toe shoes.

But luckily for her, she heard some loud noise coming from Jillian and Cornelia's open bedroom window on the second floor of the manor.

"This is the ugliest tutu trim I've ever seen!" Jillian screamed.

"And this is the cheapest and yuckiest hair ribbon that I've ever seen in my whole life!" Cornelia yelled.

Then all of a sudden, to Ballerella's sheer delight, a steady stream of ribbon and tutu fabric flew out of the window and right into her hands.

"If they don't want it, I'll gladly use it! Hooray!" Ballerella cheered, and knew she had her toe shoe ribbons.

Several hours passed, and the time for the ballet performance was approaching. Stepmother called the coach to the front door, and grinned with pride as her two awkward daughters walked down the grand staircase in their tutus and toe shoes, ready to impress the Prince.

Jillian wore a forest green tutu and leotard with orange feathers in her hair, and a blue sash around her neck. Cornelia wore a bright red leotard and short yellow tutu covered with black polka dots.

Just as the three were about to board the coach, Ballerella came running down the stairs calling, "Wait for me! Hold the coach!"

Ballerella was wearing a gorgeous and shiny pink leotard and matching tutu trimmed with pink ribbons. She also had on her brand new toe shoes she made that afternoon out of the saddle leather. They were beautifully tied up her legs with the prettiest pink ribbons that landed in her hands that afternoon.

"Oh Ballerella. What is it this time?" Stepmother grumbled.

"Oh Stepmother, I'm all ready now to dance ballet for the Prince!" called Ballerella.

"Have you done all your chores, my child? I will not tolerate any unfinished housework," Stepmother replied.

"Oh yes! The floors are shiny, the cows are milked, and your clean laundry is in your dresser," Ballerella answered.

"Very well then. Come along, child," Stepmother sighed, taking a very close look at Ballerella's beautiful new tutu and toe shoes.

"*But Mother?*" Jillian cried, stomping her foot.

"Honestly, Mother! How could you let Ballerella go to the ball and perform for the Prince? She's a terrible dancer, you know!" Cornelia wailed, tugging at her tight tutu.

Then Stepmother pointed right at Ballerella's tutu fabric, and motioned for Jillian to take a closer look.

"Oh my gosh! That's my precious tutu trim! You're a bad thief, Ballerella!" Jillian shrieked.

"Oh! And that's my best hair ribbon on Ballerella's toe shoes! Mother, she stole it from me!" Cornelia cried.

"I'm very, very disappointed in you, Ballerella. But I always knew you were a dishonest child. You may not go to the ballet tonight. And hand me those toe shoes at once," Stepmother ordered, with her mean frown.

"Yes, Stepmother. Sorry," Ballerella sighed, handing over her precious new toe shoes.

"Thieves will never be rewarded," Stepmother announced, and then threw the two leather toe shoes to Harry, her pet bulldog.

Harry caught the toe shoes in his mouth and ran off to his favorite corner to chew on them all night.

Ballerella was crushed and ran out to the barn to cry, burying her head in a haystack.

Stepmother and her two very spoiled daughters rushed off in the coach to the palace. And Ballerella was left all alone in the barn with her animal friends.

Then suddenly, a bright pink light appeared before Ballerella.

Poof!

There appeared a beautiful ballerina with a magical halo of pink light around her. She had long, curly golden hair, and wore a sparkling purple tutu and matching purple toe shoes.

"Oh, who are you?" Ballerella asked, wiping away her tears.

"I'm Kaylee, your Fairy Dancemother. You haven't much time to get to the ballet! Hurry, child!"

"But I'm not going to the ballet. I have no toe shoes, and my tutu is soaked with tears," replied Ballerella.

"That's right. You need a coach," said the Fairy Dancemother.

And then the magic happened. With the flick of her silver wand, Kaylee the Fairy Dancemother turned a pumpkin into a coach, and Ballerella's mice friends into beautiful white horses!

"*Plié, plié, plié!*" Kaylee sang the magic spell, and waved her wand back and forth.

"Oh, what a beautiful coach! Thank you so much!" Ballerella exclaimed.

"No problem. Have a good time at the ballet. I'm off now," Kaylee said.

"But wait! Um, didn't you forget something?" Ballerella asked, looking down at her bare feet.

"Oh yes! Your tiara! *Plié, plié, plié!*"

Then a beautiful diamond tiara appeared on Ballerella's head.

"Oh my, thank you! But aren't you forgetting something else?" Ballerella hinted.

"Oh where is my head today? Why of course. You need a sparkling ballet tutu and matching toe shoes. *Plié, plié, plié!*" sang Fairy Dancemother.

And then it happened. Ballerella was transformed from a tear-soaked housemaid into a beautiful ballerina! She was now wearing a gorgeous light blue tutu covered in crystals, and a pair of glass toe shoes on her tiny feet.

"Oh my goodness! I never thought I could ever look like this! It's a dream come true!" Ballerella gushed.

"My dear Ballerella, enjoy your time tonight, but be sure that above all else, you are back home by the stroke of midnight. For my magical spell is only temporary, and all will be as it was before, when the clock strikes twelve!" Fairy Dancemother warned.

And then in the blink of an eye, she disappeared in the moonlight.

Then Ballerella's horsedrawn carriage rushed her straight to the royal palace in a hurry.

The palace ballroom was filled with ballerinas from all over the kingdom, and the Prince watched them dance from his private balcony.

Young, unmarried ballerinas in tutus of every color performed in the center of the floor for the Prince. But after each performance, he yawned. And by the time Jillian and Cornelia performed their clumsy and terrible sister dance for the Prince, he thought the evening would not bring a single beautiful dancer suitable to become his princess.

The Prince yawned again, and Jillian and Cornelia ran to cry in their mother's dress over not winning the Prince.

The night was almost over, and just as the Prince was about to leave the ballet, he saw a beautiful ballerina for the first time that evening.

It was Ballerella! She was standing in the doorway in her sparkling blue tutu and glass toe shoes.

The crowd parted way for Ballerella to dance in the center of the floor.

Ballerella was nervous because she had never danced in public before. But her beautiful tutu and magical shoes gave her the strength to perform.

She curtseyed gracefully to the Prince, and then danced a graceful solo across the floor and made beautiful *arabesques* and perfect *pliés*.

The crowd stared at Ballerella as she entertained them and took their breath away. The Prince fell instantly in love with Ballerella and her beautiful dancing. Then he rushed downstairs to meet the beautiful girl he had never met before.

He bowed to her and she curtseyed, and they waltzed to the music of the Royal Orchestra.

Ballerella fell in love with the Prince, and that night was the most wonderful night of her life.

But before he could ask her name, the loud ding-dong of the royal clock rang through the palace as the clock struck midnight.

"Oh dear, I must leave!" Ballerella called, breaking away from the Prince's arms right in the middle of their waltz.

"But, but . . ." the Prince protested.

"I must head home! It's almost midnight! I'll never forget this magical evening," Ballerella promised.

"Neither will I," the Prince whispered to himself, as he watched Ballerella run out the palace door.

Ballerella ran as fast as she could back to her coach before it could turn back into a pumpkin. She tripped going down the palace stairs, but picked herself up to run again. In the rush, she left behind one of her glass toe shoes.

The Prince ran after her, calling:

"But what is your name?"

It was too late, though. Ballerella was off in her coach, racing home before her horses turned back into mice and her tutu turned back into rags.

The Prince looked down at the stairs and found the only thing left of Ballerella: her glass toe shoe.

The very next day, the Prince ordered the Royal Duke and the Royal Messenger to visit the house of every unmarried ballerina in the kingdom to find the owner of the tiny glass toe shoe.

The Royal Duke and Royal Messenger visited many houses, but not a single maiden's foot could fit into the tiny glass toe shoe. The Royal Duke was afraid he would not find his Prince's true love.

They had only one house left to try in the kingdom. It was Ballerella's house, far into the countryside that was their last visit.

"*Knock, knock, knock!*" went the front door.

"Ballerella! Get the door!" Stepmother yelled.

"Yes, Stepmother," Ballerella replied, and answered the door.

There she stood in front of the Royal Duke and his messenger, with the glass toe shoe resting on a purple pillow.

"Get out of my way, child! This is important!" Stepmother barked, pushing Ballerella to the side. "Do come in, your Royal Dukeship."

"Thank you, good lady. I'm here on official royal business to find the owner of this glass toe shoe. The Prince has announced that he will marry the girl whose foot fits this shoe."

"Oh my goodness, oh my goodness! I'm going to be the Princess!" Jillian cried, tumbling down the stairs.

"No you're not! *I'm* going to be the Princess!" Cornelia fought, leaping over Jillian and rushing to the Duke.

"Girls, behave yourselves. Now Jillian, you first," Stepmother ordered.

"If this shoe fits your foot, you will be the next Princess," the Duke told Jillian.

"Look! A perfect fit!" Jillian declared, with her heel shoved into the glass toe shoe, and her toes wiggling in the air.

"Not a fit. Next," said the Duke.

"Then it's me! I have tiny feet!" called Cornelia, as she attempted to squeeze her fat foot into the glass toe shoe.

Not only did Cornelia's rather large foot not fit into the tiny glass toe shoe, but in the process of trying it on, she accidentally kicked the messenger and made the glass toe shoe fall to the floor and break into a million pieces!

"You clumsy fool. Now all is lost," Stepmother scolded Cornelia, with a look of disgust.

"Oh no! Now the Prince will never find his true love, and I have failed him. The kingdom will be sad forever," the Duke declared.

"Wait, I'm his true love!" Jillian cried, falling to the floor, and trying to put the broken pieces of the shoe together.

"No, I'm his true love! I'll get the glue!" Cornelia screamed, pushing her sister aside and grabbing the pieces.

But just as the Royal Duke and his messenger were about to turn around and leave the house, Ballerella stepped forward and softly said:

"But wait, your royal Dukeship! Look, I have the other toe shoe. It is me you are looking for. It is me who the Prince has fallen in love with. And it is me who has fallen in love with the Prince."

"Then there shall be a grand royal wedding! And the kingdom is saved forever. Come with me to the palace, where you shall live forever in luxury and happily ever after," the Duke said, bowing to the new Princess.

Ballerella left her mean stepmother and stepsisters behind, never to see them again. And soon, Ballerella married the Prince, and she became the happiest Ballerina Princess in all the land.

The Ballet Friends Present

Snow Tights and the Seven Dancers

By Kitty Michaels

Inspired by The Brothers Grimm's
Snow White

Princess Snow Tights

Snow Tights and the Seven Dancers

Once upon a tutu in a castle beside a deep forest, there lived a beautiful young princess named Snow Tights. She had dark brown hair which shined in the sunlight, red lips the color of cherries, and the lightest white ballet tights the color of snow.

Snow Tights was a princess who loved to dance ballet. She danced in the castle, and in the gardens, and even in the middle of supper.

But Snow Tights wasn't the only dancer in the castle.

Her evil and wicked stepmother, the Queen, also danced ballet. But she had a mean heart. Every morning standing at the ballet barre, the wicked stepmother peered into her mirror and asked:

"Ballet mirror on the wall, who is the most graceful of them all?"

And the ballet mirror would always reply, "My faithful Queen, it is you, the most graceful of them all."

The Queen loved hearing she was the most graceful dancer, but one day the mirror had a different answer.

"Ballet mirror on the wall, who is the most graceful of them all?" she asked.

"My faithful Queen, you are quite graceful, but not the most graceful of them all. It is Snow Tights who is the most graceful of them all."

The Queen was so angry that she practiced ballet all day and all night for twenty-five days, in order to become the most graceful dancer once again.

But on the twenty-sixth day, the mirror said, "Snow Tights is the most graceful of them all."

So the wicked Queen came up with an evil plan. She was determined to rid her castle of Snow Tights forever, and become the most graceful dancer.

The next morning, high in the castle tower, Snow Tights was awakened with a loud knock on her door.

"Snow Tights my dear, rise and shine. Today is a very big day for you," the Queen announced, entering the bedroom.

"Good morning, Stepmother. Isn't it a beautiful morning?" Snow Tights yawned, stretching her arms.

"Pack your things quickly, as you are to have a long journey today. I have graciously decided to allow you to study ballet at the best ballet school. However, it is very far away," the Queen said.

Snow Tights was so excited to study ballet that she packed her belongings just as her stepmother said, and quickly entered the awaiting coach, just as her stepmother said.

The coachman nodded to his Queen, and yanked hard on the horse's reins to take off in a hurry.

Snow Tights rode in the royal coach. But she had no idea that the Queen had secretly ordered the coachman to drive Snow Tights far into the forest, and then to leave her there so she would never dance again.

So the coachman drove and drove, and they went deeper and deeper into the forest. And after the castle was far from sight, the coachman stopped at a deserted clearing.

"I'm sorry, Snow Tights. But I have my orders," he said, taking Snow Tights out of the coach, and placing her on a tree stump.

"Where are we? This isn't a ballet school," Snow Tights asked.

"No, it is not. And you are never to dance again. Hand me your ballet slippers," he ordered.

Snow Tights did as she was told, and removed her ballet slippers from her feet. She sadly gave them to the coachman, forming tears in her eyes.

The coachman took off, and left Snow Tights all alone in the deep, dark forest.

"Oh my! I am all alone in this scary forest, without any shoes. What am I to do? I am so scared. I shall start walking back to the castle," she decided.

And Snow Tights did walk, and walk, and walk, and walk, but she never reached the castle. She was lost and getting hungry, and had nowhere to sleep that night.

But after walking a little more, she spotted a very small house with smoke coming out of the chimney. It was much smaller than the castle. In fact, it was almost too small for her.

But as Snow Tights approached the tiny house, she heard a familiar tune that reminded her of home.

It was her very favorite ballet music that she practiced to every morning at her barre.

"Oh my! How lucky I am to find a ballet class in the middle of the forest!" she cheered.

Then Snow Tights let herself in, and took first position at the barre. But the barre was only as high as her knee.

The ballerinas and the ballet teacher in this very special ballet school were all very small, dwarf ballerinas. The barre was just the right height for them.

The tiny ballet teacher was the first to speak.

"Excuse me, fair girl, but are you in the right studio?" she asked.

"Oh Madame, please let me take class with you. I am all alone in the forest, and have nowhere else to go. I will earn my keep. I will sweep the studio floor, and I will wash the studio mirrors, and I will work very hard for you. Please let me stay and dance with you," Snow Tights begged.

"I cannot deny anyone the wish to dance ballet. You may stay. But you have no ballet slippers. This is a problem," the teacher said.

Just then, all the seven little dancers huddled together and whispered quietly to each other. Snow Tights was afraid that they did not want her there, and were thinking of a way to get rid of her, just as her evil stepmother had done.

Then one of the tiny dancers popped her head up and came forward to Snow Tights.

"We shall make you a pair of ballet slippers. We welcome you to our studio and want you to stay. Let us introduce ourselves," she said.

"I'm Klutzy," the second one said.

"I'm Dizzy," the third one said.

"I'm Messy," the fourth one said.

"I'm Sleepy," the fifth one said.

"I'm Grouchy," the sixth one said.

"I'm Fancy," the seventh one said.

"And I'm Smarty," the first dancer concluded.

"Well it is very nice to meet you all! My name is Snow Tights, and I thank you very much for being my new friends," Snow Tights said.

And they did make wonderful friends. In a few days, the dancers finished sewing Snow Tights a new pair of ballet slippers. And for many, many days they had a wonderful time, and danced to beautiful ballet music in the tiny ballet studio in the middle of the forest.

But all of their happiness would soon come to an end.

Across the forest and in the castle, the wicked Queen was once again in front of her ballet mirror, standing at the barre. And since she had banished Snow Tights from the castle and had her ballet slippers locked in a steel box deep in the castle's dungeon, she thought it would be safe to ask her favorite question.

"Ballet mirror on the wall, who is the most graceful of them all?" she asked.

"My faithful Queen, it is still the young Snow Tights," replied the mirror.

Outraged, the wicked Queen ordered the magic ballet mirror to show her where Snow Tights was dancing more gracefully than her.

And the mirror obeyed, and showed her the small house deep in the forest, and Snow Tights dancing with the seven dancers.

"So my first plan failed. I will not give up so easily. I have another plan," the Queen said to herself, and disappeared to her dressing room.

Later that day, the Queen disguised as an old woman selling ballet slippers, climbed on her horse and rode deep into the forest. She rode straight to the little ballet school, and was sure that this time she could stop Snow Tights from dancing forever.

Snow Tights was alone in the little house, as the seven dancers and their ballet teacher were out buying fabric for new tutus. She was sweeping the studio floor, just as she said she would to earn her keep. But then she heard a knock.

Knock, knock, knock!

"Oh, who could it be?" Snow Tights asked, and rushed to the front door.

She opened the door to the sight of an old woman carrying a round basket full of beautiful, rainbow-colored ballet slippers.

"Ah, my pretty! You are in luck today. I have all these beautiful ballet slippers, and I am too old to dance. You must take these slippers and put them on right away, and you will look so lovely," the stranger said.

"Oh, thank you ever so much! I just love to dance! And I just love rainbow ballet slippers!" Snow Tights cheered, accepting the basket of slippers.

"Good girl," the stranger said.

"They're so pretty, but how will I ever repay you?" Snow Tights asked.

"Try one on for me, and that will be all I want," the stranger replied, with an evil grin and mean, watchful eyes.

Snow Tights chose the pair of violet ballet slippers and quickly put them on her feet, and turned to leap into the studio to dance all afternoon. But then there was the sound of a crash.

Snow Tights had fallen to the floor, and she could not get up!

"*Ha, ha, ha, ha, ha!* You fool! Those shoes were cursed by my evil spell, and for so long as you remain the fallen princess, you shall never dance again!" the Queen yelled, and then let out a deep, loud cackle. "*Ha, ha, ha, ha!*"

Then the Queen turned around and rode back to the castle, knowing she was the most graceful dancer of them all.

Princess Snow Tights was lying on the floor crying, and unable to stand, as the Queen's cursed slippers were forever bound to her feet. They made her legs too weak to stand, and far too weak to dance.

A little while later, the seven dwarf dancers and their ballet teacher came home and found Snow Tights helpless on the floor.

"Oh my dear, why are you lying on the floor? And why are you crying?" the teacher asked.

And Snow Tights told them all about the wicked Queen and her evil spell, and how she would never dance again as long as she remained the fallen princess.

All the tiny dancers began to cry, as they had become very good friends with Snow Tights and knew she loved to dance. They sat down on the floor next to Snow Tights, and thought and thought about how to help her.

"I'll think in my sleep," said Sleepy.

"And I will think in my messy tutu," said Messy.

"Oh, I don't want to think. But I will," said Grouchy.

But even with their help, Snow Tights was still very sad and cried into the shoulder of the tiny ballet teacher.

It was very quiet while everyone was thinking and sitting around Snow Tights. But in the distance a faint sound could be heard.

Clop, clop. Clop, clop.

And then it got louder.

Clop, clop! Clop, clop!

"I have an idea," said Smarty. "Let's go ask for help."

"Great idea!" everyone sang.

And so Smarty went out front to try to get the attention of the unknown horseback rider about to pass by.

"Help, help!" Smarty cried, waving her arms.

"Whoa!" yelled the rider, stopping his horse and coming to a halt.

"Help, help!" Smarty repeated.

"What is the problem, little one?" he asked.

"Oh sir, oh sir, my friend is in trouble! Please come inside. The evil spell must be broken or Snow Tights will never dance again," she explained.

"I shall do whatever I can," said the handsome stranger.

Inside the studio, the stranger caught his first glimpse of Snow Tights, and instantly fell in love with her. It did not matter to him that she was cursed and could not even stand.

"I love you, Snow Tights. You shall be my bride," he said, kneeling to her side.

And then they were married right there on the studio floor by the tiny ballet teacher. At the end of the ceremony, they shared a sweet kiss.

"It does not matter, my bride, that you cannot stand. I love you for who you are and for your beauty, and so will all your royal subjects. For I am King Henry, and you are my new Queen!" he exclaimed.

"The spell! The spell must be broken! You are no longer the fallen princess, as you are a Queen! Stand, Snow Tights! Stand!" the ballet teacher cried.

And it was true! The spell was broken and Snow Tights rose to her feet. She did her first *pirouette* as Queen Snow Tights and dazzled her friends with a beautiful dance.

With the King's love and protection, Snow Tights would forever be safe from her evil stepmother, and free to dance ballet every day.

Snow Tights bid farewell to her new friends, and rode off into the sunset with the King.

And they lived happily ever after.

The Ballet Friends Present

Goldilocks and the Three Barres

By Kitty Michaels

Inspired by Robert Southey's
The Three Bears

Goldilocks crying and lost in the forest

Goldilocks and the Three Barres

Once upon a tutu there was a little girl named Goldilocks, whose blonde hair was as light as gold. She was a beautiful little ballerina and just loved to dance.

Every morning before her ballet class, Goldilocks went into the woods to catch butterflies in her net.

But one particular morning before ballet class, there were no butterflies for her to catch.

So Goldilocks walked a little farther into the woods, but still there were no butterflies to catch.

Goldilocks was very determined to find at least one butterfly to catch in her net, so she decided to walk a little farther into the forest.

But after walking and walking a while, Goldilocks stopped before a great oak tree and realized she had never seen it before.

"Oh no, I'm lost!" Goldilocks said to herself.

Then Goldilocks started to cry for fear of being lost. But she picked her chin up when she caught a glimpse of something in the distance. She was hoping it would be someone to help her find her way back home.

It was a house. A small house, right there in the middle of the forest, near the great oak tree.

Goldilocks hoped that someone was home so they could tell her how to find her way back. And maybe they would have some food to give her, as she had no breakfast that morning.

Knock, knock, knock.

But there was no answer.

So Goldilocks let herself into the little house. There in the main room was a beautiful and empty ballet studio.

It had gleaming wood floors, lots of sunshine, and big tall mirrors on the walls. Also on the walls were three ballet barres. One high, one middle, and one quite low.

"Ooh, I love ballet! And I love to stand at the barre!" Goldilocks cheered.

She loved to practice the five ballet positions every day in her ballet class. She had a nice teacher at home, and would practice in the little house today to make her teacher proud.

Stepping up to the ballet barres, Goldilocks stood up straight, put her hair back in a small ballet bun, and assumed first position. Then she lifted her right leg up in the air, and tried to put it up on the high barre.

"Ooh, my leg won't reach this tall barre," said Goldilocks, and put her leg back down.

Then Goldilocks tried again and put her leg on the low barre.

"Ooh, much too low. I cannot use such a low barre," she said.

Then Goldilocks tried the last barre, which was the middle one, and stretched her leg out comfortably on it.

"Ooh, just right! This ballet barre is perfect for me. I shall stretch my legs," she said.

After a few minutes of warming up at the barre, Goldilocks was all ready to dance ballet.

"Oh rats! What am I to do? I have walked barefoot all this way, and have no shoes or slippers to dance in today."

But then Goldilocks saw something hanging on the wall. It was three pairs of ballet slippers, each hanging on a nail.

So Goldilocks sat on a small stool, and tried on the first pair of ballet slippers.

"Oh my! These shoes must be for a giant. My feet will never be big enough to wear these shoes. I will certainly trip and fall in them," she said.

So Goldilocks returned the first pair of ballet slippers onto the nail, and tried on the second pair.

"*Ouch!* These ballet slippers are way too small. There's no room for my toes!" she cried.

So Goldilocks returned the second pair of slippers, and hoped the third pair would fit her feet.

And they did. Goldilocks tried them on, and they fit just right.

Goldilocks danced and danced in the ballet studio, after stretching at the barre, and finding a pair of ballet slippers that fit just right.

"Ooh, how I wish I had a tutu! It would be so much fun to dance in a tutu!" she called.

Goldilocks danced some more, but then she tripped and fell, and found herself on the floor in front of a dresser with three drawers.

"Oh, what must be in these dresser drawers?" she wondered. "It would be so nice if there was a tutu in one of these drawers."

And once again, Goldilocks was right. The dresser was in fact full of tutus. One in each of the drawers.

Goldilocks opened the first drawer and pulled out a very large tutu. She stepped into it, and stood straight up. But it was so big, it fell right to the floor.

So Goldilocks picked up the tutu, and put it back in the first drawer, and closed the drawer.

Then she opened the second drawer and pulled out a second tutu.

"Oh my, what a cute little tutu!" she cheered.

But the second tutu was very little, and when Goldilocks tried to put it on, she couldn't even get it up over her knees.

"Oh my, I hope the third drawer has a tutu as well," Goldilocks frowned.

Then she put the tiny tutu back into the middle drawer.

Goldilocks closed her eyes, crossed her fingers, and wished there would be a tutu in the third drawer, and that it would fit her perfectly.

"Ooh, I hope this one fits!" she said.

Then she opened the third drawer, and to her delight, there was a third tutu! She tried it on, and it fit just right.

So Goldilocks was happy. She was all warmed up from stretching at the barre, she was wearing ballet slippers that fit her feet perfectly, and she was wearing a beautiful tutu that fit just right.

She danced and danced, and hummed herself a little ballet tune. She did many graceful *pliés,* and also many graceful *arabesques.* And just like her teacher told her, she ended her dancing with a lovely ballet curtsey.

Oh my, had Goldilocks tired herself out! She did so much walking that morning deep into the forest, and so much ballet that afternoon in her new ballet studio, that Goldilocks made a big yawn.

And then she did another big yawn, and another bigger yawn. Oh my, was Goldilocks a sleepy girl!

So she took off her beautiful tutu, and left it lying on the floor. And she removed her pretty ballet slippers and left them on the floor, too. Then she went walking around the house to look for somewhere to take a nap.

Soon she saw a little staircase that led upstairs to a little room. She climbed the stairs, one by one, and found herself in a cozy bedroom. There she found three beds, each made up so very nicely with soft blankets and feather pillows.

Goldilocks yawned again and crawled into the first bed. She tried to sleep, but she just rolled and rolled and could not sleep a wink.

"This bed is far too hard! I could never sleep in a bed so hard," she said.

So sleepy Goldilocks got out of the first bed, and walked a few steps to crawl into the second bed. She crawled under the covers, placed her head on the pillow, and closed her eyes to take a nice nap. But there was something wrong. She was sinking in the bed!

"Oh dear, this bed is far too soft! I could never sleep in a bed this soft."

So Goldilocks yawned once again and slowly tip-toed to the third bed, and crawled right in.

"Ah, this bed is not too hard, or too soft. This bed is just right," she said.

And Goldilocks fell fast asleep, and had a nice, long rest.

A little while later, the owners of the house returned. They were three ballerinas who lived in the house and practiced in their dance studio every day. It was time for them to practice ballet, so they went straight into the studio to warm up at the barre.

The first ballerina walked over to the high barre and did her stretches. Her name was Jessie. She was very tall, and had long, long legs.

The second ballerina was Megan. She too had long legs, but not as long as Jessie's. She stretched out on her middle barre, and was ready to dance, when the third ballerina let out a shriek.

"What is it, little Lexi? What is wrong today?" Jessie and Megan asked the third and shortest ballerina.

"Someone's been using my ballet barre! Look, it's all bent!" Lexi cried, pointing to the low barre that Goldilocks had tried earlier that day.

"Hmm. Someone's been using my barre, too. It's bent, but not as bent as yours," Jessie, the tall ballerina, said.

"Oh my! Someone's been using my barre, too. It's bent *more* than yours," Megan, the middle ballerina, said.

"Well, who ever used our barres also tried on our slippers!" tall Jessie announced, grabbing her ballet slippers off their nail, and seeing they were dirty on the bottom.

"My friend Jessie, someone has tried on my slippers as well!" little Lexi called, looking at her slippers which were also very dirty on the bottom.

"Look! Someone used my slippers so much that they're lying on the floor and are black on the bottom!" Megan wailed.

"Well, who ever danced at our barres and wore our slippers has also been in our tutus!" tall Jessie announced, and walked over to the dresser.

She opened the first drawer, and found a blonde hair on her large tutu.

"Look, someone with blonde hair has tried on my tutu!" Jessie cried.

"And look! My tiny tutu is all stretched out! Someone has tried on my tutu, too!" little Lexi called.

"*Wah!*" went Megan. "Look! My tutu is lying on the floor! Someone wore my tutu and threw it on the floor! *Wah!*"

Then the three ballerinas were so tired from their hard day that they decided to skip their ballet practice and go right to bed. They were very, very tired.

But when they went upstairs to their bedroom, Jessie announced:

"Someone's been sleeping in my bed. I always make my bed, and it's so messy."

"Well, who ever has been sleeping in your bed also took a nap in mine. It's all sunken in," Lexi said.

"Well, Jessie and Lexi, who ever slept in your beds has slept in mine, too. And I know who it is! It's her!" Megan cried, ripping the covers off of little Goldilocks and waking her right up.

"*Eek!*" Goldilocks yelled, and sprang out of bed, and ran down the stairs and out the door, and all the way home.

"What a bad little girl," Jessie said.

"I agree. She did not ask permission before using our studio," Megan said.

"Or our shoes," Jessie said.

"Or our tutus," Lexi said.

"Or our beds," Megan added.

"If only she had asked our permission first, we would have said yes. And we could have all been friends. I hope she learned her lesson to ask for permission first," Jessie said, and went to her bed and finally took her nap.

And Goldilocks never took anything again without asking for permission.

The Ballet Friends Present

The Klutzy Duckling

By Kitty Michaels

Inspired by Hans Christian Andersen's
The Ugly Duckling

Kaylee the klutzy duckling

THE KLUTZY DUCKLING

Once upon a tutu there was a little ballet school house filled with children learning ballet. They were all hard at work practicing for their end of the year recital of *Swan Lake*.

There were all sorts of children in the ballet class. There were the best dancers, there were the good dancers, and then there was Kaylee.

"Kaylee, you klutz!" her classmates would call every single day.

But it was true. Kaylee was a klutz when it came to ballet.

She loved ballet and tried very hard. But her little legs would not do as she told them to do. She tried to leap, but would fall on the floor. And she tried to twirl, but only made herself dizzy.

"Okay, class. Now bend down and touch your toes," the ballet teacher told her students.

Then all the little girls touched their toes, but Kaylee stretched her arms up reaching for the sky.

"Kaylee, you did it wrong!" yelled her classmate Jill, with her head upside down, as she touched her toes.

"Kaylee, you klutz!" yelled her other classmate named Courtney.

"I'm sorry. I am such a klutz," Kaylee admitted.

"Now class, stand up straight and stretch out your arms, and reach for the sky," the ballet teacher said.

Then all the little girls reached for the sky, but Kaylee bent down and touched her toes.

"Kaylee, you did it wrong again!" Jill yelled once more.

"Kaylee, you klutz!" Courtney sang.

"Class, don't make fun of Kaylee. She can't help being a klutz," the teacher said, shaking her head at Kaylee.

Then the ballet class formed a line to have their outfits checked by the teacher. One by one, the teacher checked each little girl's pink tights, black leotard, and neat ballet hair bun.

Every girl passed the test, except for Kaylee, who was last in line.

"Kaylee, do you always have to look different? Why are you wearing an orange leotard? And why is your hair down and so messy? And why are you wearing no tights at all?" her teacher asked.

"I'm sorry. I am such a klutz," Kaylee sighed, looking down at her feet and forming a frown.

"*Ha, ha!* Kaylee, go home! You don't belong here!" Jill called, and pointed at the door.

"Now class, Kaylee is quite a klutz, but just maybe with a lot of hard work, she could one day become a beautiful and graceful ballerina," the teacher said.

"Kaylee? Not a chance," declared Bianca, the pretty, blonde dancer.

"She should go home. Her orange leotard sticks out like a sore thumb," Jessie, the tallest dancer, agreed.

"Yeah, I'm not the best, but I'm better than Kaylee!" Megan, the silly ballerina, laughed.

"Class, that is enough for today. I will see you again tomorrow," the teacher said.

Out the door all the little girls went. And the very next day, they came right back through the very same door.

They stood at the ballet barre and bent down to touch their toes, and once again Kaylee reached for the sky.

"Kaylee, you did it wrong!" Jill yelled.

"Kaylee, you klutz!" Courtney teased.

"I'm sorry. I am such a klutz," Kaylee sighed, and then bent down to touch her toes, but instead bumped into Jill and knocked her over.

"*Ouch!*" cried Jill. "You don't belong here! Just go home!"

And the class agreed.

But the ballet teacher gave Kaylee one more chance.

They lined up again in their leotards, and the teacher once again praised every student for wearing the proper ballet uniform. Except for one little girl at the end of the line, whose name was Kaylee.

"Kaylee, why are you still wearing your orange leotard? And why is your hair down and so messy?" the teacher asked.

"I'm sorry. I'm such a mess. I'm such a klutz. Maybe I don't belong here," Kaylee frowned.

Then the class laughed, and took turns teasing Kaylee.

"Kaylee, you'll never be in the recital! You can't play a duckling!" Jill called.

"Kaylee, you klutz! You can't be one of us!" Courtney yelled.

"You're just a klutzy duckling!" Bianca declared.

"Yeah, you can't dance with us!" Jessie added.

"Nope, not in a million years!" Megan laughed.

"But everyone gets to play a duckling," Kaylee said. "Why can't I? Can't I dance with the rest of the class?"

Then the teacher said:

"Kaylee, I'm afraid the class is right. If you don't learn to be like the other ducklings, then you can't play one at all. There's no room for a klutzy duckling in the ballet."

"You're right. I *am* a klutzy duckling. I'll go home now," Kaylee frowned, and headed for the door.

The class cheered and watched Kaylee pick up her dance bag, take off her ballet slippers, and head for home.

But in the hallway, Kaylee bumped into a little ballerina waiting for her class to begin.

"*Ouch!* You bumped into me!" the little brown-haired ballerina cried.

"I'm sorry. I am such a klutz. I do it all the time," Kaylee admitted.

"That's okay. I'm fine. My name is Lexi. What's yours?" the girl asked.

"Kaylee the klutz," she replied.

"Really? Why?" Lexi asked.

"Well, I do everything wrong and fall down. And I don't have the right color leotard," Kaylee explained.

"Really? I like your orange leotard. But you could easily get another to fit in with the rest of the class. And why do you fall down when your legs are so long? They're much longer than mine. You could be really good at ballet, if you tried," Lexi said.

"*Really?* You think I could be good? You think I have ballet legs?" Kaylee asked.

"Sure. Look at me. I'm so short! You can leap much higher than me. Let me tell you a secret," Lexi said.

"What? I want to know the secret. I want to be a beautiful ballerina. Please tell me the secret," Kaylee said.

"Okay. Here it is. If you believe in your heart that you are a beautiful ballerina, and if you practice every day, you will surely become a beautiful ballerina. You just have to believe in yourself and practice every day!" Lexi told her.

"But I'm a klutz," Kaylee insisted.

"Only if you think you are," Lexi wisely said.

"Thank you very much for telling me the secret! I'll go home now and believe that I'm a beautiful ballerina, and maybe, just maybe, I'll come back and I won't be a klutzy duckling," Kaylee decided.

"Yeah!" Lexi nodded and smiled.

Then Kaylee smiled back and headed straight for home.

For the rest of the week, Kaylee was absent from ballet class. Everyone thought that Kaylee had quit, and they even took her name off the cast list for the recital.

Her ballet teacher was sad that she was gone, but was very busy teaching the other little girls how to dance like ducklings for the recital.

But Kaylee did not really quit.

She was home practicing harder than she had ever practiced before.

She practiced bending down and touching her toes, and reaching up for the sky, and dancing in a straight line.

After all her hard work, Kaylee began to feel less klutzy. She became very good at dancing like a duckling.

But she still didn't look right. She knew she needed to put her long, messy hair in a ballet bun, and buy a black leotard and pink tights for class.

So Kaylee went to the dance store and bought herself the proper ballet uniform, and tucked her old orange leotard away in a drawer.

And for her messy hair, she invited her new friend Lexi over to her house, and asked her to teach her how to make a ballet bun. She just never knew how to make one before.

Very soon, Kaylee was no longer a klutzy duckling. And she also had a nice new friend, who didn't call her a klutz.

"Kaylee, you're a beautiful ballerina," Lexi told her, as she walked with her to class the next Monday.

"Thank you, Lexi. You've been such a help. I don't even recognize myself," Kaylee said.

"Just remember to believe in yourself, Kaylee. And know that you're *not* a klutz," Lexi reminded her.

"Thank you, Lexi. I will," Kaylee said, and smiled.

"Good luck!" Lexi called, and watched Kaylee go into class.

With her head held high and her shoulders back, and wearing her new black leotard, pink tights, and long hair neatly tied in a bun, Kaylee gracefully walked into class.

Then she took her place at the barre.

"Oh, who is that beautiful ballerina?" Jill asked, looking right at Kaylee.

"I don't know. But she's pretty and very graceful!" Courtney called.

"Ooh, I like her leotard! How pretty it is! It looks just like mine!" admired Bianca.

"And her legs are even longer than mine!" Jessie noticed. "Her leaps must be higher than mine!"

"Gosh, she makes me look bad," Megan sighed, looking at the new student from head to toe.

"Class, don't you recognize who this girl is? Why it's Kaylee! Your old friend! But she can't play a duckling in the recital. She must play the Swan!" the teacher declared.

"*Really?* I will play the Swan?" Kaylee asked.

"Yes, with your newfound grace and beautiful dancing that I see you have practiced, you will surely play the Swan," the teacher replied.

Then Kaylee stepped out in front of the class, and did the most beautiful *pirouette* she had ever done in her whole life!

The class cheered for their new Swan, and would never, ever call Kaylee a klutzy duckling again.

MEET THE CAST

Come backstage and meet the cast! The characters you just read about also star in *Ballet Friends,* the ballet book series by Kitty Michaels.

Bianca: The beautiful and fancy ballerina who loves to host parties and give presents to her friends. You met her as Princess Bianca in "The Princess and the Prima." She also played the roles of Ballerella and Goldilocks.

Jessie: The graceful and talented ballerina who loves to perform in recitals. You met her as the Prima in "The Princess and the Prima." She also played the tall ballerina in "Goldilocks and the Three Barres."

Megan: The funny and smart ballerina who loves to spend time with her friends and make them laugh. You met her as the Chambermaid in "The Princess and the Prima." She also played the middle ballerina in "Goldilocks and the Three Barres."

Lexi: The small and sweet ballerina who loves to play music and dance all day. You met her as the piano player in "The Princess and the Prima," and also as Snow Tights in "Snow Tights and the Seven Dancers." She also played the helpful friend in "The Klutzy Duckling."

Kaylee: The cute and clumsy ballerina who loves animals and cooking food for all her friends. You met her as the Fairy Dancemother in "Ballerella." She also starred as herself in "The Klutzy Duckling."

Turn the page for a special preview of Ballet Friends #1 Toe-tally Fabulous!

Ballet Friends

Toe-tally Fabulous
#1

Chapter One
Beginning

1

best foot forward

"I got in! I'm gonna dance in Paris! *Yippee!*" Bianca Best sang, twirling around her room with a special letter from Paris in her hand.

Bianca just got invited to the Paris Pirouette program. It was an amazing ballet school for gifted young dancers in beautiful Paris, France.

Bianca was eleven, and had light blonde hair and sky blue eyes. She just finished fifth grade last week. And now she couldn't wait to move to Paris and start school there in September.

"That's right, Bianca bear, but it says in your letter that you need fifty hours of official pre-pointe ballet class before you can go," her mom said, sitting down on Bianca's pink canopy bed.

"Yeah, I just did the math on my calculator. If I go to ballet camp every day for the whole summer, I'll have exactly the right amount of hours. Things couldn't be more perfect!" Bianca figured.

"Oh gumdrops! Your first hour of class starts really soon. Are you all set to go?" her mom asked.

"Yeah, Mom. Check me out!"

Then Bianca twirled around for her mom. She was wearing a light purple leotard that was covered in sparkly pink and purple crystals.

"Look, I'm *toe*-tally fabulous! I can't wait to try on my toe shoes today!" Bianca cheered.

"Maybe you'll change your mind about going to Paris?" her mom hoped, reading the letter.

"I'll miss you too, Mom. But it's only for a year. Wow, I can't believe I'm going to Paris to be a real prima ballerina! It's a really good thing I'm starting pre-pointe today," Bianca said.

"Oh my gosh, I'm so proud of you. Meet you downstairs," her mom said.

"It's time for my lucky bun!" Bianca called, pulling out a secret gold box from under her bed.

Then she unlocked the box with a key she kept under her pillow. Inside, she found ten ballet buns just waiting to be put on her head.

"Eeny meeny miny moe. Catch a tiger by his toe, or toe shoe. He, he!" Bianca giggled, pointing to the biggest bun in the box.

Then she stuck it on top of her own bun, and pinned it down with some bobby pins.

"*I'm fabulous! And I'm Bee-on-ca!*" she sang, twirling in front of the mirror.

Then she topped off her outfit by placing a real diamond tiara on her head.

"This is gonna be the best summer ever! I can't believe I'm starting *pointe* today!" Bianca cheered.

After a five minute ride in her mom's white Mercedes SUV, Bianca arrived for ballet camp at the Ridgepoint Community Center.

It was a big white mansion on Main Street with pretty rose gardens, a grand ballroom for weddings, and a ballet studio on the top floor.

"Mom, don't I look *toe*-tally fabulous? I *am* learning toe today. Actually, *toe*-day!" Bianca joked, admiring her tiara in the car mirror, and undoing her seatbelt.

"You do look fabulous! You're my ballet star! You're so sparkly today," her mom giggled.

"That's because it's show time!" Bianca cheered, hopping out and carrying a bunch of pink balloons and a box of hot cinnamon buns.

She pranced right into the mansion, and couldn't wait to get the ballet party started.

Then the white SUV drove off, and next to arrive was a blue Volvo wagon with a license plate which read: "BRACES."

"Megan, we're late. Look, Bianca Best already got here. Oh no, I wanted you to walk in together," Mrs. Fields said to her redhead daughter.

"Tell Dad. He's like the busiest orthodontist ever. My whole school was sitting in the waiting room. Why can't I just cut in line? I *am* his own kid," Megan joked, flashing a mouth-full of braces with hot pink rubber bands.

"Megan, just run in. And remember, the faster you run, the more calories you burn. And don't forget you have your clogging lesson after ballet."

"*Gosh, can't a girl just get a summer break?*" Megan whined.

"Oh Megan. Just be happy I couldn't get you into that new circus trapeze class," her mom said.

Then Megan let out a big chuckle, and ran to ballet class with her dance bag.

Off went the blue Volvo wagon, and up next was a tan Honda mini-van with classical music bursting out of the windows.

It was the Levin family performing one of their regular violin concerts, right there in their Honda!

The mini-van's sliding door opened, and a small girl named Lexi (short for Alexis) jumped down to the sidewalk. She carried her violin case, and skipped up the steps to the Community Center. Her brown ponytail danced around as she bounced in.

Then suddenly, behind the mini-van, appeared a large white truck with a food counter and menus stuck to the side. It sat there for a couple minutes, filling the air with smoke. Finally, a girl with curly brown hair hopped out of the back of the truck and rolled into the bushes.

Made in the USA
Middletown, DE
19 September 2019